P9-BZS-370

RIDGEFIELD LIBRARY
472 MAIN STREET
RIDGEFIELD, CT 06877
(203) 438-2282
www.ridgefieldlibrary.org

NOV 17
2020

Usha was born under a gray sky.

In her town, the sun hadn't shone for as long as anyone could remember.

Anyone, that is, but her grandfather.

When Grandfather was little, he played in the sun,

from the moment it
climbed into the sky...

until it dropped
back down at night.
Everyone did.

"Where did it go?" Usha asked as she settled in for one of Grandfather's many stories.

"One day," he explained, "they built the biggest wall we'd ever seen, brick by brick. And it blocked out the sun."

"Why, Grandfather?"

"I couldn't imagine why. But I was only a child."

"Who, Grandfather? Who were they?"

"They were the people who made the rules."

"Why didn't you yell and scream and make them stop?"

"We did yell, Usha," whispered Grandfather.
"But they were unmoved."

Each time her grandfather told the story, it became harder and harder for him to remember.

"It's been too long, my Usha," Grandfather told her. "I'm afraid I will never feel the sun again."

Usha decided to do something.

Working from her
grandfather's stories, Usha began
to walk east in search of the sun.

On the first day, she saw clouds pouring
rain into puddles as big as swimming pools.

On the second day, she walked through
a forest of fog as thick as soup.

On the third day,
Usha saw something that
stopped her in her tracks.
She gave it a sniff.

Was this the smell of sunshine?

Usha hurried onward until night fell.
Exhausted, she laid her blanket next to an
enormous rock and fell asleep.

The next morning, Usha opened her eyes.
She couldn't believe what she saw.
It wasn't a rock she was curled against, but a wall.

Usha pushed the wall.

She kicked the wall.

And she tried, without any luck at all, to climb the wall.

Finally, Usha faced the wall and said,
"Wall, I have come all this way, now move."

The wall didn't respond.

"WALL," said Usha, louder this time,
"you are in my way, now MOVE."

Nothing happened.

"WALL!" Usha shouted at
the top of her lungs.

"MOVE."

A brick began to wiggle.

"Who said that?" asked a voice from behind the wall.

Usha imagined one of the people from her grandfather's stories.

"I AM USHA."

The brick stopped moving.

Then Usha saw another brick shift back and forth. "Why are you yelling?" asked another voice.

"I AM HERE FOR THE SUN!" Usha shouted.

The brick was rammed back into place.

Out of breath, Usha remembered what Grandfather had told her:
He *had* yelled, but they were unmoved.

Usha studied the wall. Then she whispered,
"I want the sun."

Several bricks began to shift.

"What did she say?" asked a boy.

"Shh! I can't hear her from behind this silly old wall," said another voice.

"I am here for the sun," Usha sang quietly into the wall.

Then she began to share Grandfather's stories. Some were sad and made Usha cry. Others were funny, and she laughed aloud. Many of the stories made Usha angry. She shared them all as brick after brick was removed.

And just as Usha was almost out of words, the wall began to shake...

The wall began to sway...

And with a giant rumble,
the wall *crashed* to the ground!

When the dust cleared, Usha climbed the pile of bricks and saw...

...children!
"She's just like us!"
one whispered.

"But now, the sun shines on me, too," said Usha.

And that moment, she felt the sun for the first time. It was warmer—brighter than words could have ever described.

Through valleys and forests, over hills
and mountains, Usha ran west.

She watched the sun peek through the clouds
and paint the gray sky away.

Finally, she saw the light stream over Grandfather's face.

Usha was home, and so was the sun.